TW♡S♡MES

Love Poems from the Animal Kingdom

poems by *Marilyn Singer*

pictures by *Lee Wildish*

Alfred A. Knopf

New York

WOODLAND PUBLIC LIBRARY

Bats

Good morning! How the nighttime flew!
Now, may I hang around with you?

Dogs

Nice to meetcha! You smell delish!
Wanna share my water dish?

Cats

A sunny day. It's perfect weather
to go outside—and nap together.

Horses

Nose to nose, hip to hip,
ours is a stable relationship.

squirrels

It's *a-corny* thing, but also true—
I like how you scamper. I'm nuts about you!

Porcupines

Hugging you takes some practice.
So I'll start out with a cactus.

Chameleons

You and I could be a team,
if we agree on color scheme.

Zebras

You dazzle me in bright sunlight—
and that's the truth in black and white.

Elephants

I like your tusks, I like your trunk.
I like your size—you're quite a hunk.

sharks

Mentally, we're an ideal match!
Dentally, you're my perfect catch!

Dolphins

Come leap with me and be my wife.
You're the porpoise of my life.

Earthworms

We're perfect together. I guarantee
that I dig you and you dig me.

Caterpillars

I'm finding a leaf. You're taking a bite.
Wait a few weeks and our hearts will take flight.

Geese

I have a hunch. I think you're ready.
Honk once for yes if you'll go steady.

Pigeons

We'll spend the day wooing, dodging the cars.
We'll spend the night cooing, under the stars.

To Debbie and Jerry, a great twosome.

And thanks to Steve Aronson; Kristine O'Connell George; my editor, Janet
Schulman, and the other good folks at Random House; and, especially, Pat Lewis,
for his inspiration.
—M.S.

THIS IS A BORZOI BOOK PUBLISHED BY ALFRED A. KNOPF

Text copyright © 2011 by Marilyn Singer
Illustrations copyright © 2011 by Lee Wildish

All rights reserved. Published in the United States by Alfred A. Knopf, an imprint
of Random House Children's Books, a division of Random House, Inc., New York.

Knopf, Borzoi Books, and the colophon are registered trademarks of
Random House, Inc.

Visit us on the Web! www.randomhouse.com/kids

Educators and librarians, for a variety of teaching tools,
visit us at www.randomhouse.com/teachers

Library of Congress Cataloging-in-Publication Data
Singer, Marilyn.
Twosomes : love poems from the animal kingdom / by Marilyn Singer ; illustrations
by Lee Wildish.
p. cm.
ISBN 978-0-375-86710-1 (trade) — ISBN 978-0-375-96710-8 (lib. bdg.)
1. Animals—Juvenile poetry. 2. Love—Juvenile poetry. 3. Children's poetry,
American.
I. Wildish, Lee. II. Title.
PS3569.I546 N67 2010   811'.54—dc22   2009037608

MANUFACTURED IN CHINA
January 2011   10 9 8 7 6 5 4 3 2 1   First Edition